◆

The Town That
Got Out of Town

◆

The Town That Got Out of Town

Robert Priest

DAVID R. GODINE · PUBLISHER · BOSTON

Published in 1989 by
David R. Godine, Publisher, Inc.
Horticultural Hall
300 Massachusetts Avenue
Boston, Massachusetts 02115

Library of Congress Cataloging-in-Publication-Data

Priest, Robert, 1955–

The town that got out of town / text and illustrations by Robert Priest
p. cm.
Summary: When the residents of Boston leave town over Labor Day
weekend, the city's buildings and landmarks decide to visit
Portland, Maine.
ISBN 0-87923-786-4
[1. Boston (Mass.)—Description—Fiction.   2. Portland (Me.)
Description—Fiction.] I. Title.
PZ7.P9343To   1989   88-46108
[E]—dc19   CIP
                       AC

FIRST EDITION
Printed in the United States of America

♦

For Helen Fernau

♦

The Town That
Got Out of Town

It was the last week of the long, hot summer, and it seemed that EVERYBODY wanted to get away for the Labor Day weekend. Everyone was getting out of town and heading for the wide open spaces of the great outdoors.

Bags all packed, families headed out.

The town animals decided they needed a vacation too, so off they went.

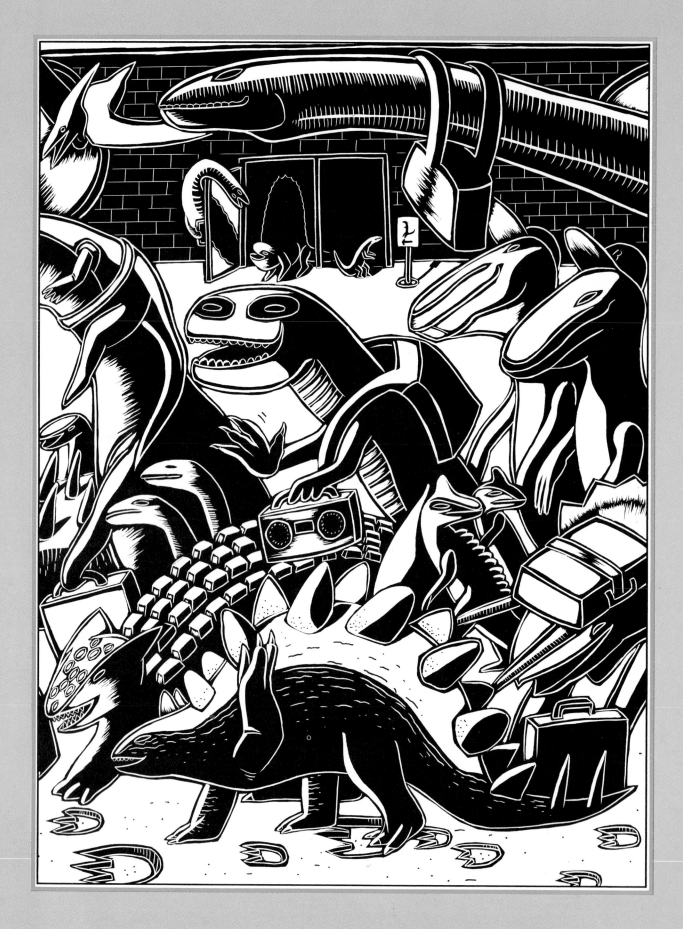

Even the dinosaurs in the museum, bored without visitors,
collected their radios, hats, and bags and left town.

Soon the streets were completely empty.

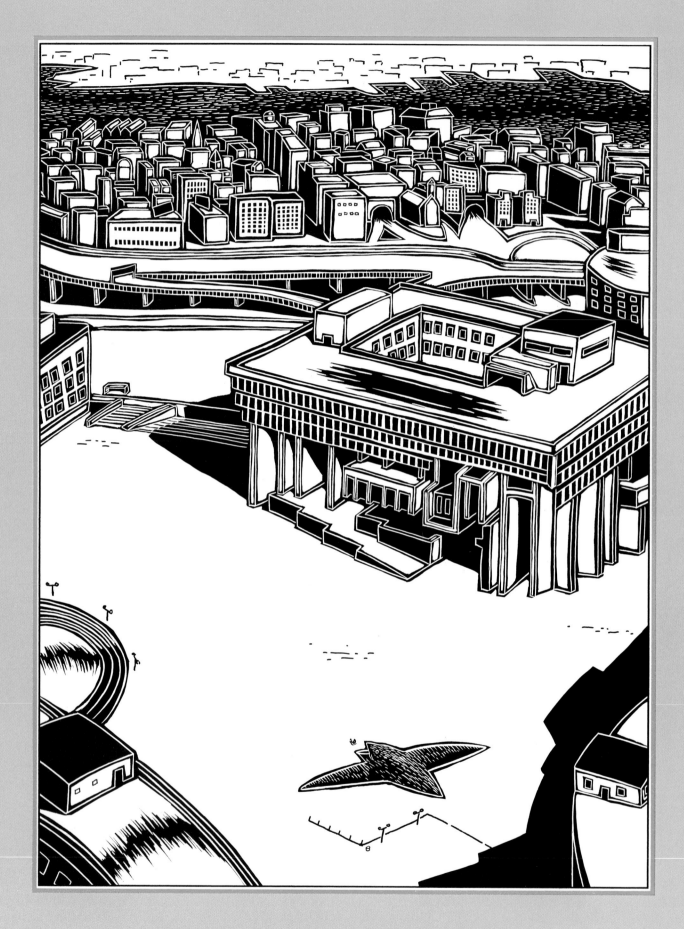

Except for one little bug and one lonely bird.

And one dog.

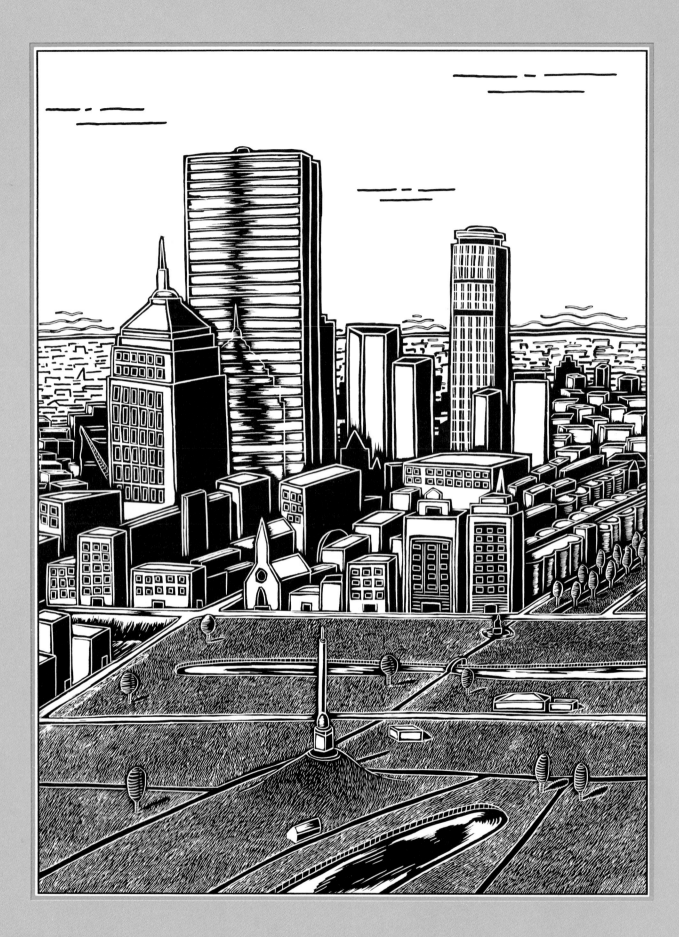

And soon even these were gone.
Only heat waves stirred in the quiet, empty town of Boston.

In the quiet of that night sat the Custom House. Feeling very alone, it began to think, and remember old friends. It thought very, very hard and soon the whole town heard and listened.

"Friends and fellow buildings. Everyone's taken a vacation
but us. You know, it's been decades since
we've seen our friends in Portland, Maine. So . . .

"Why don't WE leave? Let's take a trip!"

And all the buildings agreed:

"Yes, Yes, let's get out of town!"

Very early the next morning the pumping station
closed the huge valves that let water flow to the city.

The power station shut off the electricity.

Then the recycling plant stopped work, too,
as there was nothing left to recycle.

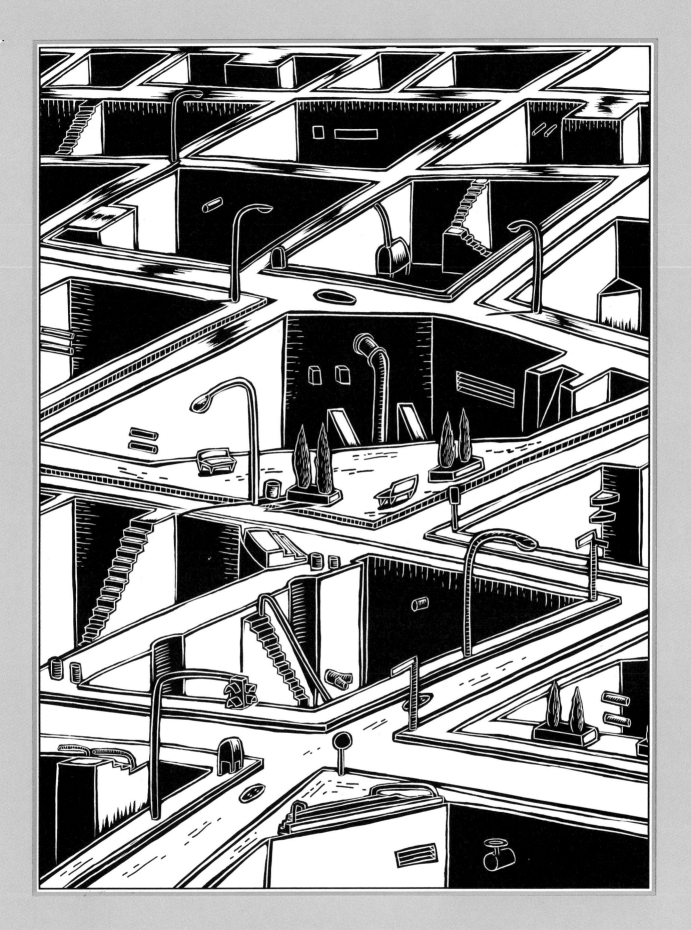

Suddenly the buildings were gone!

They had been very careful not to break anything as they left.

As falcons hovered above the dunes, the buildings began
their trip up the coast—with their windows closed, of course.

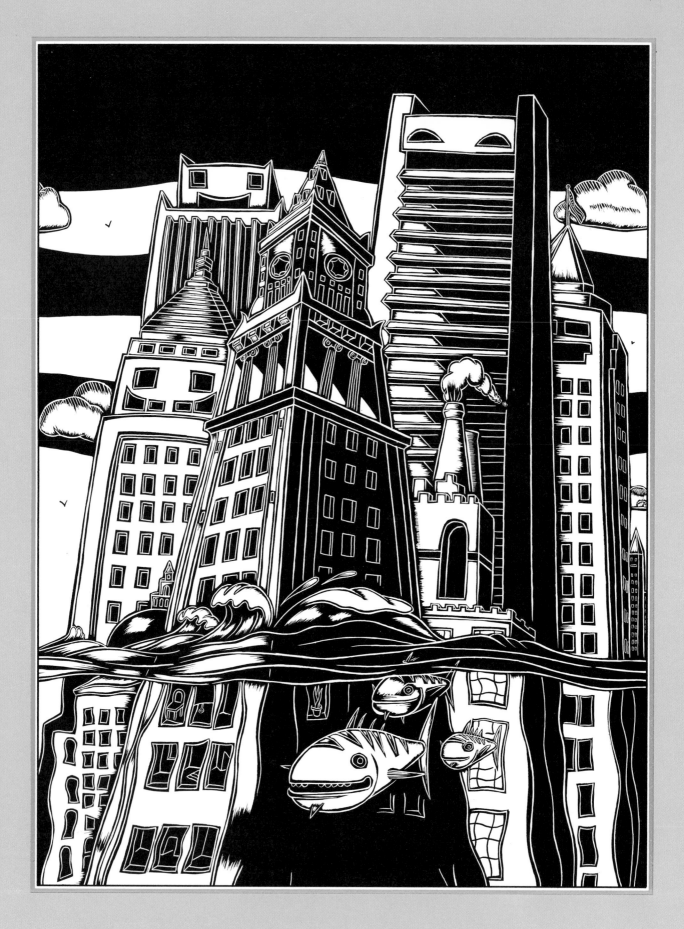

Some friendly fish followed along for a while.

Around noontime they passed through farm country.
It was turning into a beautiful day.

They traveled through deep woods as well,
full of whispering trees and calling birds.

Like all travelers, they crossed many bridges.

That afternoon, as the town came to the top of a hill, the Custom House saw Portland. "SURPRISE!" Portland was *very* surprised.

"Look, it's Boston!" exclaimed Portland. "How good to see you; it's been years. Time sure flies when you're a town."

All the people had left Portland too, so the whole town was theirs.

When all the new buildings had been introduced, old friends
went visiting. The old State House went to see the Longfellow House;

the museums traded pieces of art. Portland was given a bust
of John Adams and Boston a painting by Whistler.

The two libraries stood close together and exchanged the latest journals.

The two tallest buildings talked about air quality
while down below the churches discussed religion.

And the Boston and Portland customhouses traded stories.
Business had been slow, but that was fine with them because
they were getting along in years and they'd seen a lot already.

As far as the eye could see, small groups of buildings

were exchanging thoughts under the blue-jay sky.

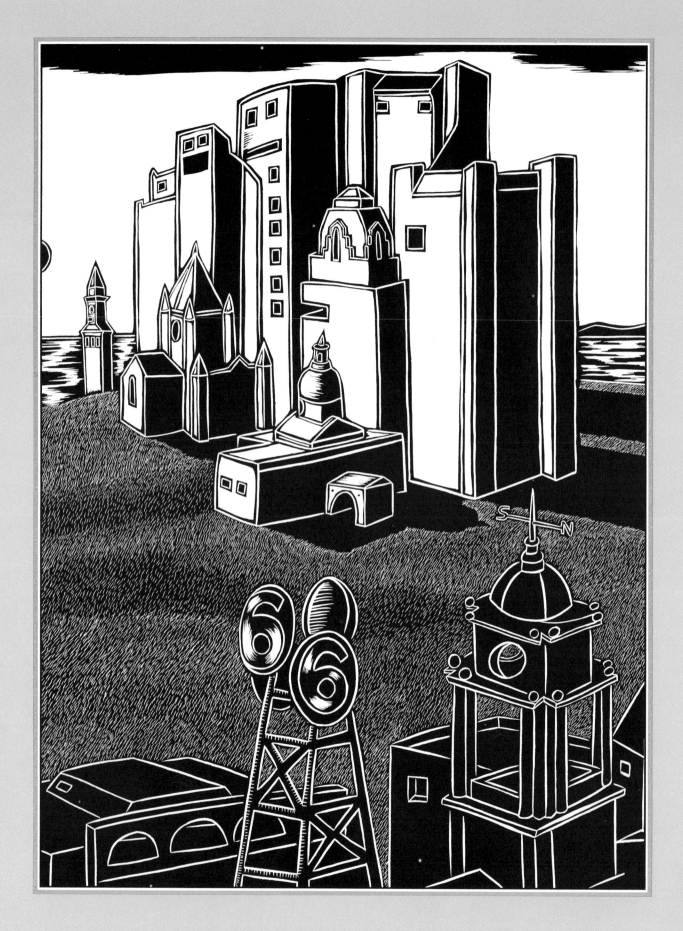

All good things *do* come to an end, and so did this vacation.
On Monday afternoon, Boston began the trip home.
"Goodbye!"
"Don't take any wooden nickels!"

Back through the woods and fields and waters the buildings
went, following the trusty Custom House.

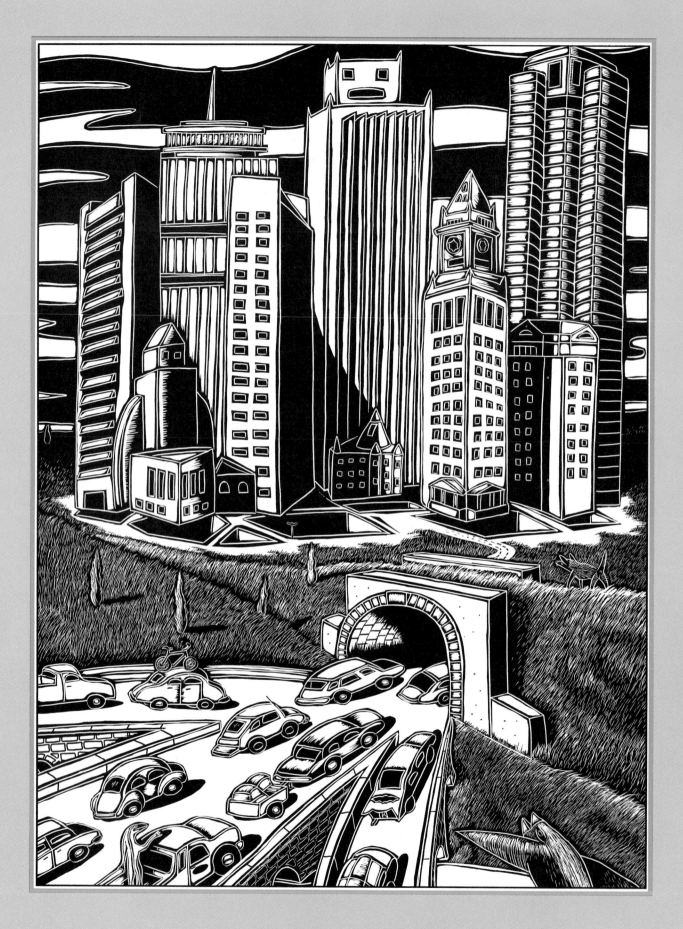

At last, just as the sun was going down, they reached home.
And not a moment too soon.
Just as the very last building was settling onto its foundation,
a dog appeared. Then a bird. And soon . . .

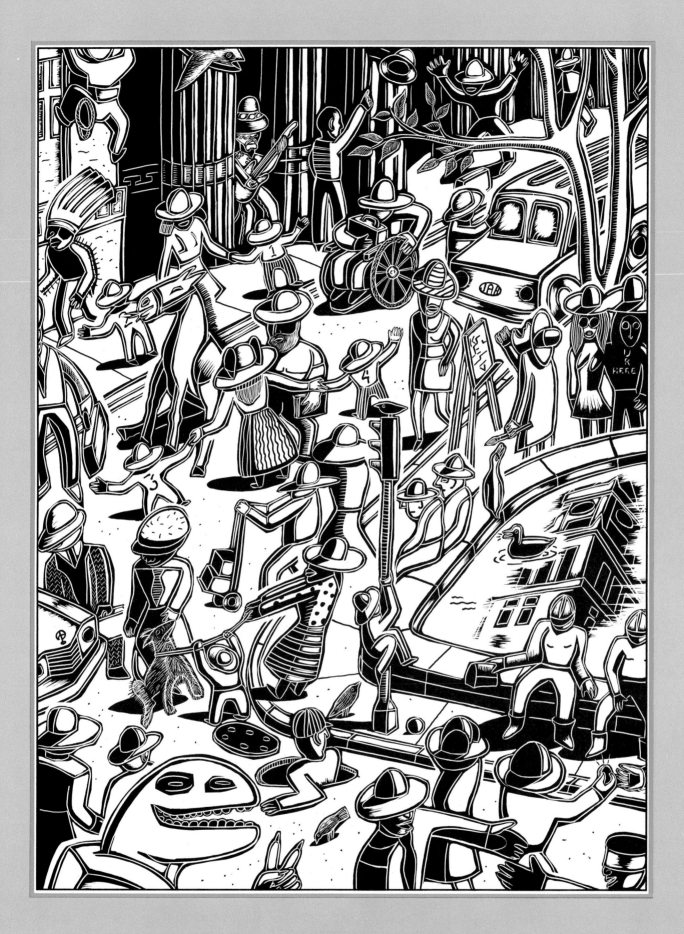

Everyone was back, rested and happy,
including the town that got out of town. And no one was the wiser.

About the author and the illustrations

ROBERT PRIEST is an illustrator and painter,
dividing his time between Boston and Limington,
Maine, contributing to many publications throughout
the New England area. The illustrations in this book were
produced on scraperboard. This process uses illustration board,
to which hard white clay has been bonded and overprinted
with a black dye. Engraving tools were used to expose
the white beneath the black surface, resembling a
linoleum or wood block print in the finished
illustration.

Designed by Lisa Clark

Printed by Holyoke Lithograph

Bound by Book Press